KB127565

허수경 시선

허수경 시선

Poems by Huh Sukyung

지영실, 다니엘 토드 파커 옮김

Translated by YoungShil Ji, Daniel T. Parker

POET

아시아

차례
Contents

허수경
시선

Poems by Huh Sukyung

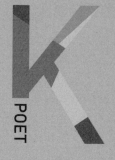

POET

혼자 가는 먼 집

당신……, 당신이라는 말 참 좋지요, 그래서 불러봅
니다 킥킥거리며 한때 적요로움의 울음이 있었던 때,
한 슬픔이 문을 닫으면 또 한 슬픔이 문을 여는 것을 이
만큼 살아옴의 상처에 기대, 나 킥킥……, 당신을 부릅
니다 단풍의 손바닥, 은행의 두 갈래 그리고 합침 저 개
망초의 시름, 밟힌 풀의 흙으로 돌아감 당신……, 킥킥
거리며 세월에 대해 혹은 사랑과 상처, 상처의 몸이 나
에게 기대와 저를 부빌 때 당신……, 그대라는 자연의
달과 별……, 킥킥거리며 당신이라고……, 금방 울 것
같은 사내의 아름다움 그 아름다움에 기대 마음의 무덤
에 나 벌초하러 진설 음식도 없이 맨 술 한 병 차고 병자
처럼, 그러나 치병과 환후는 각각 따로인 것을 킥킥 당
신 이쁜 당신……, 당신이라는 말 참 좋지요, 내가 아니
라서 끝내 버릴 수 없는, 무를 수도 없는 참혹……, 그러
나 킥킥 당신

I Go Alone to a Distant Home

You ⋯, the word 'you' sounds very good so I call you giggling   Once there was a cry of solitude as one sadness closed its door and another sadness opened its   Leaning on my wound caused by having lived so long I *tee-hee* ⋯, call 'you'   A maple palm, the cleft of a gingko leaf, then the reunion, the flea-bane's anxiety, the trampled grass returns to the soil You ⋯, I'm giggling about time or love and wounds, when a wounded body rubs against mine   You ⋯, you are nature's moon and star ⋯, I'm giggling, it's you ⋯,   The beauty of a guy near tears, leaning on that beauty I head to the grave of my mind to cut the weeds with only a bottle of alcohol hanging from my hip and no food to arrange at the grave[1]   Like a sick person but healing a disease and having a disease are two different things *tee-hee* you lovely you ⋯, the word 'you' sounds so good because it isn't me   I can never abandon the misery or ask for a refund ⋯, but *tee-hee* you

1 Korean people regularly visit their family members' graves to cut down weeds and participate in a ceremony that includes an offering of food and drink to the deceased.

不醉不歸

어느 해 봄그늘 술자리였던가

그때 햇살이 쏟아졌던가

와르르 무너지며 햇살 아래 헝클어져 있었던가 아닌가

다만 마음을 놓아보낸 기억은 없다

마음들끼리는 서로 마주보았던가 아니었는가

팔 없이 안을 수 있는 것이 있어

너를 안았던가

너는 경계 없는 봄그늘이었는가

마음은 길을 잃고

저 혼자

몽생취사하길 바랐으나

가는 것이 문제였던가, 그래서

갔던 길마저 헝클어뜨리며 왔는가 마음아

나 마음을 보내지 않았다

더는 취하지 않아

갈 수도 올 수도 없는 길이

날 묶어

Bul-Chwi-Bulg-Wi [2]

Was it a drinking party under a spring shadow one year?
Did sunshine gush down then?
Was I crashed and tangled under the sunshine? Wasn't I?
Yet I don't remember releasing my mind

Did our minds face each other? Didn't they?
Something may be hugged without arms
so did I hug you?
Were you the boundless spring shadow?

My mind got lost
and alone
wished to die drunkenly, living in a dream
but maybe going was the problem, so
did it come tangling the same path it went down earlier?

2 According to a story from the Joseon Dynasty, at a banquet for the workers constructing historic Hwaseong Fortress in Suwon, King Jeongjo the Great told them "Bul-chi-mug-wi" (basically the same meaning as the title) which means "If you don't get drunk, you can't leave."

더 이상 안녕하기를 원하지도 않았으나

더 이상 안녕하지도 않았다

봄그늘 아래 얼굴을 묻고

나 울었던가

울기를 그만두고 다시 걸었던가

나 마음을 놓아보낸 기억만 없다

I didn't release my mind
Without being drunk anymore
I was stranded
on the way I couldn't come or go
so I didn't want to be fine anymore
but I wasn't fine anymore either

Did I cry
with my face buried under the spring shadow?
Did I stop crying and walk again?
I remember it all except the part about releasing my
mind

공터의 사랑

한참 동안 그대로 있었다
썩었는가 사랑아
사랑은 나를 버리고 그대에게로 간다
사랑은 그대를 버리고 세월로 간다
잊혀진 상처의 늙은 자리는 환하다
환하고 아프다
환하고 아픈 자리로 가리라
앓는 꿈이 다시 세월을 얻을 때
공터에 뜬 무지개가
세월 속에 다시 아플 때

몸 얻지 못한 마음의 입술이
어느 풀잎자리를 더듬으며
말 얻지 못한 꿈을 더듬으리라

Love in an Empty Lot

After being still for so long
has love rotted?

Love leaves me and goes to you
Love leaves you and goes to time

An old scar from a forgotten wound is bright
Bright and hurting

I will go to that bright hurting spot
at the instant the ill dream is revived

at the instant a rainbow that appears in an empty lot
feels pain again inside time

lips in my mind that never found a body
will grasp at a dream that never found words
will grasp at green grass

흰 꿈 한 꿈

혼자 대낮 공원에 간다

술병을 감추고 마시며 기어코 말하려고

말하기 위해 가려고, 그냥 가는 바람아, 내가 가엾니?

삭신은 발을 뗄 때마다 만든다, 내가 남긴 발자국, 저
건 옴팍한 속이었을까, 검은 무덤이었을까, 취중두통의
길이여

고장난 차는 불쌍해, 왜?

걷지를 못하잖아, 통과해내지를 못하잖아, 저러다 차
는 썩어버릴까요

저 뱀도 맘이 아파, 왜?

몸이 다리잖아요 자궁까지 다리잖아요 그럼,

얼굴은 뭘까?

사랑이었을까요……

아하 사랑!

마음이 빗장을 거는 그 소리, 사랑!

부리 붉은 새, 울기를 좋아하던 그 새는 어디로 갔나요?

그런데 왜 바보같이

White Dream Single Dream

I go alone at midday to a park
drinking from a concealed bottle   Certainly, I go
in order to speak; wind, you don't bother me, do
you feel sorry for me?

The path of my hangover headache
Each time I lift my feet my muscles and joints leave
footprints behind me   Are they hollow interiors?
Black graves?

Why do I feel sympathy for a broken-down car?
It can't move, can't transport, as things go, will it rot?
Why does that snake also make my mind hurt?
Its body is a leg   Its womb is part of the leg   Then
what is the face?
Maybe it is love ...
Aha love!
The sound of the mind deadbolting its door, love!

Where did the red-beaked bird that liked to cry go?
By the way why did I, like a fool,

벌건 얼굴을 하고 남몰래 걸어다닐 수 있는 곳만 찾아
다녔지?

그 손, 기억하니?

결국 마음이 먹은 술은 손을 아프게 한다

이 바람……

내 마음의 결이 쓸려가요 대팻밥 먹듯 깔깔하게 곳간
마다 손가락, 지문, 소용돌이, 혼자 대낮의 공원

햇살은 기어코 내 마음을 쓰러뜨리네

당신……

look only for places I could walk in secret with my
red face?

Do you remember my hand?
The drink my mind had ends up hurting my hand
This wind ...

The texture of my mind is swept away   Every storage room, fingers, fingerprints,
  swirls, being alone at midday in the park, all soaked
and gritty as if absorbing
  wood shavings

Certainly, sunshine smashes into my mind

You ...

너의 눈 속에 나는 있다

나는 그렇게 있다 너의 눈 속에

꽃이여, 네가 이 지상을 떠날 때 너를 바라보던 내 눈
속에

너는 있다

다람쥐여, 연인이여 네가 바삐 겨울 양식을 위하여 도
심의 찻길을 건너다 차에 치일 때

바라보던 내 눈 안에 경악하던 내 눈 안에

너는 있다

저녁 퇴근길 밀려오던 차 안에서 고래고래 혼자 고함
을 치던 너의 입안에서

피던 꽃들이 고개를 낮추고 죽어갈 때

고속도로를 달려가다 달려가다 싣고 가던

얼어붙은 명태들을 다 쏟아내고 나자빠져 있던 대형
화물차의

하늘로 향한 바퀴 속에 명태의 눈 안에

나는 있다

나는 그렇게 있다 미친 듯 타들어가던 도시 주변의 산

I Exist Inside Your Eyes

I exist like this inside your eyes
Flower, as you leave this earth, inside my eyes that
gazed at you
you exist
Squirrel, my lover, as you rush across the downtown streets
for food in winter and are run over by a car
inside my witness eyes, my shocked eyes
you exist

Alone, you yell at the top of your lungs in your car
on the way home
in the evening rush hour
blooming flowers bow their heads and perish in
your mouth
Your tractor-trailer truck speeds and swerves on an
expressway
tumbles and pours out its load of frozen Alaskan
pollack
inside the wheels turned to the sky, inside the eyes
of the fish
I exist

림 속에

　오래된 과거의 마을을 살아가던 내일이면 도살될 돼
지의 검은 털 속에

　바다를 건너오던 열대과일과 바다 저편에 아직도 푸
르고도 너른 잎을 가진

　과일의 어미들 그 흔들거리던 혈관 속에

　나는 있다 오래된 노래를 흥얼거리며 뻘게를 찾는 바
닷가

　작은 남자와 그 아이들의 눈 속에 나는 있다 해마다

　오는 해일과 홍수 속에 뻘밭과 파괴 속에

　검은 물소가 건너가는 수렁 속에

　과거에도 내 눈은 그곳에 있었고

　과거에도 너의 눈은 내 눈 속에 있어서

　우리의 여관인 자연은 우리들의 눈으로

　땅 밑에 물 밑에 어두운 등불을 켜두었다

　컴컴한 곳에서 아주 작은 빛이 나올 때

　너의 눈빛 그 속에 나는 있다

　미약한 약속의 생이었다

　실핏줄처럼 가는 약속의 등불이었다

I exist inside a forest near a city that burns insanely

Inside the black hair of a pig to be slaughtered to-morrow in an old village

Inside the swaying blood vessels of tropical fruits crossing the ocean

and their mothers with wide green leaves on the other side of the ocean

I exist inside the eyes of a short guy and his kids who hum an old song

as they search for three-spined crabs on the shore I exist

inside tsunamis and annual floods on the mudflats and destruction

inside a quagmire as a black water buffalo crosses

Also in the past my eyes were there

Also in the past your eyes were inside my eyes

Nature, our inn, using our eyes

left dark lanterns lit underground under water

When the slightest light gleams from a pitch-dark place

I exist inside the expression of your eyes

It is the life of a faint promise

It is the lantern of a promise as thin as a small vein

글로벌 블루스 2009

울릉도산 취나물 북해산 조갯살 중국산 들기름
타이산 피쉬소스 알프스에서 온 소금 스페인산 마늘
이태리산 쌀

가스는 러시아에서 오고
취나물 레시피는 모 요리 블로거의 것

독일 냄비에다 독인 밭에서 자란 유채기름을 두르고
완벽한 글로벌의 블루스를 준비한다

글로벌의 밭에서 바다에서 강에서 산에서 온 것들과
취나물 볶아서 잘 차려두고 완벽한 고향을 건설한다

고향을 건설하는 인간의 가장 완벽한 내면을 건설한다
완벽한 내면은 글로벌의 위장으로 내려간다

여기에다 외계의 별 한잔이면 글로벌의 블루스는 시

Global Blues 2009

Ulleungdo[3] *chwinamul*[4] North Sea clam meat Chinese perilla[5] oil
Thai fish sauce salt from the Alps Spanish garlic Italian rice

Gas comes from Russia
and the *chwinamul* recipe is from a cooking blog

I put canola oil grown in a German's field in a pot made in Germany
and prepare a perfect global blues

I set a neat table with stir-fried *chwinamu*l and things that came from global fields oceans rivers mountains and build a perfect hometown

I build the most perfect interior of a human who builds a hometown

3 Ulleungdo is a South Korean island located 75 miles east of the peninsula.
4 Aster scaber herb that has culinary and medicinal uses.
5 A plant of the mint family that is a common feature of Korean cuisine.

작된다

　고향의 입구는 비행장 고향의 신분증은 패스포트

　오 년에 한 번 본에 있는 영사관으로 가서 패스포트를
갱신하는

선택이었다 자발적인 유배였으며 자유롭고 우울한
선택의 블루스가 흐르는 세계의 중심부에서 변방까지
불선택의 블루스가 흐르는 삶과 죽음까지

글로벌이라는 새 고향, 블루스를 울어야 하는 것이다

이 가난의 고향에는 우주도 없고 이 가난의 고향에는
지구에 사는 인간의 말을 해독하고 싶은 외계도 없다

다만 블루스가 흐르는 인공위성의 심장을 가진
바람만이 있다 별 한잔만이 글로벌의 위장 안에서 진다

The perfect interior goes down into the global stomach

Now if I take a drink from a distant star the global blues will begin

The hometown's entrance is an airport the ID card of the hometown is a visa

I go to the consulate in Bonn once every five years to renew my visa

Voluntary exile was my choice
through the center of the world and the frontier
the blues of my free but gloomy choice flow here
the blues of no choice flow through life and death

I should cry the blues for my new global hometown

The hometown of my poverty is not a cosmos

The hometown of my poverty is not outer space that wants to decipher
the language of a human living on the earth

Blues flow in the wind with the heart of a manmade satellite

Only the drink from a distant star falls into my global stomach

비행장을 떠나면서

비행장을 떠나면서 나는 울었고 너도 울었지
비행장을 떠나면서 사람들은 커피를 마시며 우울한
신문들을 읽었고
참한 소설 속을 걸어다니며 수음을 했지
사랑이 떠나갔다는 걸 알았을 때 사람들의 가슴에서
는 사막이 튀어나왔는데
사막에 저리도 붉은 꽃이 핀다는 건 아무도 몰라서 꽃
은 외로웠지

비행장을 떠나면서 사람들은 테러리스트들을 향해
인사를 했고
비행장을 떠나면서 지상에 쌓아놓은 모든 신문들에
게 불안한 악수를 청했어
울지 마, 라고 누군가 희망의 말을 하면
웃기지 마, 라고 누군가 침을 뱉었어

21세기의 새들은 대륙을 건너다가 선술집에 들러 한
잔 했지

At the Airport Exit

At the airport exit I cried and you did too

At the airport exit people read gloomy newspapers and drank coffee

while muttering to themselves and walking in their nice fictions

When people realized love had left them deserts bloomed from their hearts

an intense red flower bloomed in the desert but none of them saw it

so the flower was lonely

At the airport exit people waved at the terrorists

and at the airport exit they anxiously held out their hands

to a pile of all the earth's newspapers

Don't cry when someone uttered hopeful words

Don't be funny another spat out

21st century birds landed in a tavern for drinks while crossing a continent

21세기의 모래들은 대륙과 대륙에 새 집을 짓다가 스
시 집에 들러
  차가운 생선의 심장을 먹었어

  21세기의 꽃게들은 21세기의 모기들은 21세기의 은
행나무들은
  인사를 하지 않는 시간을 위해 오랫동안 제사를 지냈지
  21세기의 남자들은 21세기의 여자들은 아이들은 소
년과 소녀들은

  비행장을 떠나면서 사랑이 오래전에 떠난 사막에 핀
붉은 꽃을 기어이
  보지 못했지, 입술을 파르르 떨며 꽃이 질 때
  비행장을 떠나면서 우리들은 새 여행에 가슴이 부풀어
  헌 여행을 잊어버렸지, 지겨운 연인을 지상의 거리,
어딘가에 세워두고
  비행장을 떠나면서 우리들은 슬프면서도 즐거웠지

21st century sands landed in a sushi bar while constructing houses in continents
and ate cold fish hearts

21st century blue crabs 21st century mosquitoes 21st
century gingko trees
held a long rite of sacrifice for time that had failed
to greet them
21st century men 21st century women children boys
girls

At the airport exit they were never able to see the
red flowers blooming
in the deserts where love left so long ago and the
flowers fell with trembling lips
At the airport exit we were buoyant with new journeys
forgot old journeys as our boring lovers stood on
some street of the earth
At the airport exit we felt sad and yet pleasant

차가운 해가 뜨거운 발을 굴릴 때

문득 나는 한 공원에 들어서는 것이다
도심의 가을 공원에 앉아 있는 것이다
이 저녁에 지는 잎들은 얼마나 가벼운지
한 장의 몸으로 땅 위에 눕고

술병을 들고 앉아 있는 늙은 남자의 얼굴이 술에 짙어
져 갈 때
그 옆에 앉아 상처 난 세상의 몸에서 나는 냄새를 맡
으며
차가운 해가 뜨거운 발을 굴리는 것을 바라보는 것이다

얼마나 다른 이름으로 나, 오래 살았던가
여기에 없는 나를 그리워하며
지금 나는 땅에 떨어진 잎들을 오지 않아도 좋았을
운명의 손금처럼 들여다보는데

몰랐네

When the Cold Sun Shifts His Hot Feet

Suddenly I'm inside a park
I'm seated in a park of downtown autumn
Nearly weightless leaves wafting in this evening
When a leaf touches the sail of its body to the ground
and

the face of the old guy sitting with a bottle in his
hand darkens from drinking
I'm seated next to this guy and can smell the body
of a wounded world
as I study him the cold sun shifts his hot feet

How long have I lived, with different names?
Missing the me who isn't here
I now study the fallen leaves as palms with lines of
their destinies
that could have been better if they had not come here

I didn't know
a shadow falls with only silence remaining at the

저기 공원 뒤편 수도원에는 침묵만 남은 그림자가 지고
　　저기 공원 뒤편 병원에는 물기 없는 울음이 수술대에
놓여 있는 것을

　　몰랐네
　　이 시간에 문득 해가 차가워지고 그의 발만 뜨거워
　　지상에 이렇게 지독한 붉은빛이 내리는 것을

　　수도원 너머 병원 너머에 서서
　　눈물을 훔치다가 떠나버린 기차표를 찢는
　　외로운 사람이 당신이라는 것을

　　나는 몰라서
　　차가운 해는 뜨거운 발을 굴리고
　　지상에 내려놓은 붉은 먼지가 내 유목의 상처를
　　물끄러미 바라보는 동안

　　술 취해 잠든 늙은 남자를 남기고
　　나는 가을 공원에서 나오는 것이다

monastery behind the park

a dry cry is placed on an operating table at the hospital behind the park

I didn't know

the sun suddenly grows cold and only his feet are hot at this time of day

so an intense red shade descends upon the earth

the lonely person

who wipes away tears and shreds the ticket of the train that has already left

standing beyond the monastery and beyond the hospital   is you

I didn't know

so while the cold sun is shifting his hot feet

and the red dust he shakes down on the earth is blankly studying

my nomadic wound

I leave the autumn park

leave the old guy behind to sleep it off

아름다운 나날

　검은 비닐봉지도 사진을 찍어놓으면
　꼭 물결치는 바다처럼 보입니다 어떤 영화에서 보았
습니다
　모래 한 바께쓰를 확대하면
　꼭 낙타가 쓰러져 죽어가는 사막처럼 보입니다 역시
어떤 영화에서
　보았습니다

　아마도
　하수구의 녹슨 파이프 속을 찍으면
　누군가 잘라낸 제 목을 들고 걷고 있는 대륙처럼 보이
지 않을까요?
　태어나기도 전에 죽어가는 어린 신부들이 살고 있는
그 대륙처럼요,
　영화에서 보았습니다

　검은 비닐봉지 바다 위에

Beautiful Days

When a black plastic bag is photographed
it looks just like a rolling sea I saw in a movie
When a bucket of sand is magnified
it looks like the desert where a camel collapses and
dies in that movie

Perhaps
if the inside of a rusty sewer pipe is photographed
will it look like a continent where someone carries
my severed head?
Like a continent where little brides live as they are
dying before being born
I saw that in a movie

On the sea on the black plastic bag
a church was constructed and from inside the new
church
I saw little brides in rubber shoes roaming and beg-
ging for *tteokguk*[6]

6 Traditional rice cake soup, a traditional New Year's Day dish in Korea

교회당이 서고 새로 세워진 교회당 속 고무신을 신고
떡국을 얻어먹으러 다니는 어린 신부들을 보았습니다.

아무도 첫 월경을 축하하지 않았습니다
첫 시험을 치르러 가는 어린 신부들
시험을 치르고 가까운 구리광산 옆에 선 중국루에서
엄마, 나 곧 돈 벌 거야, 라고 어린 신부들은 말합니다

어이, 마누라 아직도 울고 있나, 라고
어린 신랑이 물어보면
여보, 우린 곧 멸망할 거야, 라고
어린 신부는 답합니다

울고 있는 어린 신부의 눈을 확대해서 찍으면
   태어나기도 전에 구걸을 하러 다니던 코끼리의 등처
럼 보이지는 않을까요?
   두터운 피부는 햇빛 아래에서 마르며 갈라졌겠지요
   다른 한편으로는
   아기 코끼리를 수렁에서 건져내던 어미 코끼리의 등
처럼 보이지는 않을까요?

No one celebrated their first menstruations

Little brides went for their first try

Went to a Chinese restaurant next to a copper mine
after the attempt

"Mom soon I will make money" say little brides

"Hey honey are you still crying?"
asks a little bridegroom
"Honey soon we will be ruined"
answers a little bride

When a little bride's crying eye is magnified and
photographed

will it look like the back of an elephant that was a
beggar before being born?

Its thick skin was doubtlessly parched and cracked
by the sun

Meanwhile

will it look like the back of an elephant pulling her
baby from a muddy bog?

I saw that it a movie

I love movies

Whenever I say that I want to cry

영화에서 보았습니다

영화를 사랑합니다

그 말을 할 때마다 울고 싶어요

사용기간이 지난 약을 그 대륙에 팔러 나선 유럽의 약

장수처럼

검은 비닐 바다를 통과해서 사막 바께쓰 속을 지프차

로 건너가던

학살자의 검은 안경처럼

울고 싶어요, 그 말을 할 때마다 영화가 보고 싶어요

누군가 우리를 수탈했어, 라고 그곳 인권운동가가 인

터뷰를 하면

누군가가 누구인가를 자꾸 묻고 있는 영화가 있었습

니다

그 영화 안에 앉아 비닐봉지 바다나 바께쓰 사막을 봅

니다

울고 싶어요

아름다운 나날입니다

like a European peddler coming to the continent to
sell expired medicines
   like the black eyeglasses of a person committing
genocide
   crossing the desert bucket in a jeep sailing the plastic bag sea
   Whenever I want to cry I want to see a movie

   There was a movie where
   a human rights activist being interviewed said
"Someone has abused us"
   Then the question "Who was it?" was persistently
demanded
   I'm in the movie and see the plastic bag sea or the
sand bucket desert
   I want to cry
   Beautiful days

그때 낙타가 들어왔다

마음에 든 소금
날 목마르게 한다
목마름이 짠 흰빛의 원천이다

그대는 먼 바다에서
죽음의 물결을 땅 쪽으로 밀어내고 있다
그때마다
나는 모래사막에 엎혀진 소금 기둥처럼 녹는다

무너진 마음집 지반 사이로
옛 사원이 떠올라
내 마음속 양초 만드는 이들은 운다

아픈 이가 느릿느릿 죽을 입안으로 넣듯
그를 간호하는 이가 시름에 겨워
아무것도 목구멍으로 넣지 못하듯
낙타는 나에게로 들어온다

A Camel Enters Me

The salt of my mind
causes my thirst
Thirst is the source of white salty light

From a distant sea you
are pushing the waves of death toward shore
Each wave
melts me like a column of salt lain on desert sands

Through a crevice in the foundation of my mind's
collapsed house
an ancient monastery arises
so candle makers inside my mind cry out

As if a sick person slowly puts a spoonful of por-
ridge between the lips
as if the caretaker who worries too much
couldn't swallow anything
a camel enters me

사막의 신기루로 꿈을 엮던 낙타

목이 말라 눈을 감을 때

사막에는 소금 열리고

낙타의 눈에도 소금이 맺힌다고 했다

나는 눈을 감고 소금을 기다렸다

그때 알았다

해갈의 기척이 저 짠 흰빛에 있다

그 빛 날 데리고 갔다

목마름이 생애의 열쇠였다

텅 빈 고방을 지키는 열쇠였다

The camel has woven a dream from the desert mi-
rage
I heard that when it closed its eyes with thirst
salt grew in the desert
salt formed in the camel's eyes

I close my eyes to wait for salt
then realize
the sign of slaking thirst is found in that white salty
light

The light takes me
Thirst was the key of my life
Thirst was the key that secured the empty *gobang*[7]

---

7 A storage building used in old days for foods, tools or other items
  that could not be stored inside the house.

빌어먹을, 차가운 심장

이름 없는 섬들에 살던 많은 짐승들이 죽어가는 세월
이에요

이름 없는 것들이지요?

말을 못 알아들으니 죽여도 좋다고 말하던
어느 백인 장교의 명령 같지 않나요
이름 없는 세월을 나는 이렇게 정의해요

아님, 말 못하는 것들이라 영혼이 없다고 말하던
근대 입구의 세월 속에
당신, 아직도 울고 있나요?

오늘도 콜레라가 창궐하는 도읍을 지나
신시(新市)를 짓는 장군들을 보았어요
나는 그 장군들이 이 지상에 올 때
신시의 해안에 살던

Damn My Cold Heart

On days when many animals on nameless islands
are dying

They are nameless, right?

Doesn't it sound like the order from a white army
officer
who said it was okay to kill the ones who couldn't
understand speech?
I define nameless days like this

Or, on days at the threshold of modern times
that said mutes don't have souls
Hey you, still crying?

Again today I saw generals building the new city
as I passed the capital where cholera is flourishing
When the generals came to the earth
I saw a baby salamander
living on the city's coastline stare at me

도롱뇽 새끼가 저문 눈을 껌벅거리며
달의 운석처럼 낯선 시간처럼
날 바라보는 것을 보았어요

그때면 나는 당신이 바라보던 달걀 프라이였어요
내가 태어나 당신이 죽고
죽은 당신의 단백질과 기름으로
말하는 짐승인 내가 자라는 거지요

이거 긴 세기의 이야기지요
빌어먹을, 차가운 심장의 이야기지요

slowly opening and closing blind eyes

as if I am a lunar meteorite, as if I am a strange time

Then I was a fried egg you were staring at

You died because I was born

I am an animal with speech growing

because of the protein and oils of your corpse

This is a story of a long century

It's a story of damn my cold heart

레몬

 당신의 눈 속에 가끔 달이 뜰 때도 있었다 여름은 연
인의 집에 들르느라 서두르던 태양처럼 짧았다
 당신이 있던 그 봄 가을 겨울, 당신과 나는 한 번도 노
래를 한 적이 없다 우리의 계절은 여름이었다

 시퍼런 빛들이 무작위로 내 이마를 짓이겼다 그리고
나는 한 번도 당신의 잠을 포옹하지 못했다 다만 더운
김을 뿜으며 비가 지나가고 천둥도 가끔 와서 냇물은
사랑니 나던 청춘처럼 앓았다

 가난하고도 즐거워 오랫동안 마음의 파랑 같을 점심
식사를 나누던 빛 속, 누군가 그 점심에 우리의 불우한
미래를 예언했다 우린 살짝 웃으며 대답했다, 우린 그
냥 우리의 가슴이에요

 불우해도 우리의 식사는 언제나 가득했다 예언은 개나
물어가라지, 우리의 현재는 나비처럼 충분했고 영영 돌

Lemon

Sometimes the moon rose inside your eyes   That
summer was as short as if the sun raced to set in its
lover's house

You and I didn't sing even once when you stayed
during other seasons   Our season was that summer

Fierce lights randomly thrashed my forehead   I
couldn't hug you sleeping even once   Simple rains
passed in hot steam and when thunderstorms visited
the stream swelled like a youth suffering from the
growth of wisdom teeth

We had poor but pleasant lunches in light which
would last as waves in our minds   Someone predict-
ed our star-crossed future and we responded with
simple smiles saying *We are only our hearts*

Despite our misfortune we always ate full meals
Sic the dogs on that prediction   The present was
plentiful and beautiful as butterflies as if it would

아오지 않을 것처럼 그리고 곧 사라질 만큼 아름다웠다

　레몬이 태양 아래 푸르른 잎 사이에서 익어가던 여름
은 아주 짧았다 나는 당신의 연인이 아니다, 생각하던
무참한 때였다, 짧았다, 는 내 진술은 순간의 의심에 불
과했다 길어서 우리는 충분히 울었다

　마음속을 걸어가던 달이었을까, 구름 속에 마음을 다
내주던 새의 한 철을 보내던 달이었을까, 대답하지 않
는 달은 더 빛난다 즐겁다

　숨죽인 밤구름 바깥으로 상쾌한 달빛이 나들이를 나
온다 그 빛은 당신이 나에게 보내는 휘파람 같다 그때
면 춤추던 마을 아가씨들이 얼굴을 멈추고 레몬의 아린
살을 입안에서 굴리며 잠잘 방으로 들어온다

　저 여름이 손바닥처럼 구겨지며 몰락해갈 때 아, 당신
이 먼 풀의 영혼처럼 보인다 빛의 휘파람이 내 눈썹을
스쳐서 나는 아리다 이제 의심은 아무 소용이 없다 당
신의 어깨가 나에게 기대오는 밤이면 당신을 위해서라

vanish quickly and never return

In a very short summer a lemon ripened among green leaves under the sun *You don't love me* I spent a cruelly short time considering my statement caused by a fleeting suspicion It lasted long enough for us to cry too much

Did the moon walk through my mind? Did the moon give one season like a bird gives its entire heart to the clouds? The moon doesn't answer only glows more brightly and is pleased

Fresh moonlight comes out for a picnic from behind a night cloud that holds its breath The moonlight feels like your whistle Now young ladies who were dancing in the village compose their faces and enter sleeping rooms while rolling sour lemon flesh in their mouths

As the summer sags and wrinkles like a palm ah you seem like the soul of faraway grasses The whistle from the light brushes against my eyebrows and I feel sour Now there is no point to my sus-

면 나는 모든 세상을 속일 수 있었다

그러나 새로 온 여름에 다시 생각해보니 나는 수줍어
서 그 어깨를 안아준 적이 없었다

후회한다

지난여름 속 당신의 눈, 그 깊은 어느 모서리에서 자
란 달에 레몬 냄새가 나서 내 볼은 떨린다, 레몬꽃이 바
람 속에 흥얼거리던 멜로디처럼 눈물 같은 흰빛 뒤안에
서 작은 레몬 멍울이 열리던 것처럼 내 볼은 떨린다

달이 뜬 당신의 눈 속을 걸어가고 싶을 때마다 검은
눈을 가진 올빼미들이 레몬을 물고 향이 거미줄처럼 엉
킨 여름밤 속에서 사랑을 한다 당신 보고 싶다, 라는 아
주 짤막한 생애의 편지만을 자연에게 띄우고 싶던 여름
이었다

picion   The night you came to put your shoulder against mine I could have deceived the whole world for your sake

In this new summer I remember I never hugged that shoulder because I was shy
Now I regret

Now I smell the lemon moon that grew in the farthest corner of your eyes last summer and my trembling cheeks are a melody of lemon blossoms that were humming in the wind my trembling cheeks are a small lemon that was hanging like a tear in my white back yard

I want to walk into your eyes where the moon rose as black-eyed owls make love by biting lemons and the scent tangles like spider webs in the summer nights   *I miss you*   That summer I wanted to send nature letters about my very short life

수박

아직도 둥근 것을 보면 아파요

둥근 적이 없었던 청춘이 문득 돌아오다 길 잃은 것처럼

그러나 아휴 둥글기도 해라

저 푸른 지구만 한 땅의 열매

저물어가는 저녁이었어요

수박 한 통 사들고 돌아오는

그대도 내 눈동자, 가장 깊숙한 곳에

들어와 있었지요

태양을 향해 말을 걸었어요

당신은 영원한 사랑

태양의 산만한 친구 구름을 향해 말을 걸었어요

당신은 나의 울적한 사랑

태양의 우울한 그림자 비에게 말을 걸었어요

당신은 나의 혼자 떠난 피리 같은 사랑

Watermelon

Seeing anything round causes me pain
My youth was never round and got lost on its way
back

But wow it is so round
The fruit from the ground is as big and green as the
earth

In the dusky evening
you were walking back with a watermelon
You were also
in the deepest part of my eyes

I talked to the sun
You are my eternal love
I talked to the cloud   the sun's distracted friend
You are my melancholy love
I talked to the rain   the sun's gloomy shadow
You are my flute-like love who left alone

땅을 안았지요
둥근 바람의 어깨가 가만히 왔지요
나, 수박 속에 든
저 수많은 별들을 모르던 시절
나는 당신의 그림자만이 좋았어요

저 푸른 시절의 손바닥이 저렇게 붉어서
검은 눈물 같은 사랑을 안고 있는 줄 알게 되어
이제는 당신의 저만치 가 있는 마음도 좋아요

내가 어떻게 보았을까요, 기적처럼 이제 곧

푸르게 차오르는 냇물의 시간이 온다는 걸
가재와 붕장어의 시간이 온다는 걸
선잠과 어린 새벽의 손이 포플러처럼 흔들리는 시간
이 온다는 걸
날아가는 어린 새가 수박빛 향기를 물고 가는 시간이
온다는 걸

I hugged the ground
The round shoulders of the wind came quietly
In those days I didn't know numerous stars
were inside a watermelon
I only liked your shadow

Knowing the red palms in these green days
clasp black tears like love
now I like your detached mind too

How could I see it? As quickly as a miracle

the time of a stream swelling in blue will come
the time of crayfish and congers will come
the time of shallow sleep and tiny hands of dawn
swaying like poplar leaves
will come
the time of a little bird flying with a watermelon-
tinted fragrance in its beak
will come

딸기

당신이 나에게 왔을 때 그때는 딸기의 계절

딸기들을 훔친 환한 봄빛 속에 든 잠이

익어갈 때 당신은 왔네

미안해요, 기다린 제 기척이 너무 시끄러웠지요?

제가 너무 살아 있는 척했지요?

이 봄, 핀 꽃이 너무나 오랫동안

당신의 발목을 잡고 있었어요

우리 아주 오래전부터

미끄러운 나비의 날갯짓에 익어가던 딸기처럼 살았지요

아주 영영 익어버린 봄빛처럼 살았지요

당신이 나에게로 왔을 때

시고도 달콤한 딸기의 계절

바람이 지나다가 붉은 그늘에 앉아 잠시 쉬던 시절

손 좀 내밀어

Strawberry

Strawberries are in season when you come to me

You come while my sleep is ripening in the bright
spring light
that steals strawberries

Should I be sorry if the hints that I was waiting for
you were so obvious?
Did I pretend too strongly that I was alive?
My spring blooms have been grabbing at your ankles
for so long

For a long time we
have lived like strawberries ripening within a but-
terfly's smooth flutterings
have lived like the eternally ripening light of spring

When you come to me
it is the sweet-and-sour season of strawberries
is the time of the passerby wind resting awhile inside red shadows

Hold out your hands
please take me

저 좀 받아주세요

푸른 잎 사이에서 땅으로 기어가며 익던 열매 같은

시간처럼 받아주세요

당신이 왔네

가방을 내려놓고 이마에 맺힌 땀을 닦네

저 수건, 태양이 짠 목화의 숨

작은 수건에 딸기물이 들 만한 저녁 하늘처럼

웃으며 당신이 딸기의 수줍은 방으로 들어와

불그레해지네 저 날숨만 한 마음속으로 지던

붉은 발걸음 하나

미안해, 이렇게 오라고 해서요

미안해, 제가 좀 늦었어요

한 소쿠리 가득한 딸기 속에 든

붉은 비운을 뒤적이는 빛의 손가락 같은 간지러움

당신이 오는 계절,

딸기들은 당신의 품에 얼굴을 묻고

영영 오지 않을 꿈의 입구를 그리워하는 계절

Take me in this season
of ripening fruit crawling in the dirt through green
leaves

You come
You plop down your bag and wipe sweat from your
brow
The towel is a breath of cotton woven by the sun
The evening sky looks like the towel soaked in
strawberry juice
You come smiling into the shy strawberry's space
and are imbued with red   A red footprint
as large as an exhalation is planted into my senses

I'm sorry I asked you to come
I'm sorry you waited so long
Tickling fingers of light rummage through red
bruises
in a basketful of strawberries

The season when you come
the season when a strawberry yearns at the threshold of a locked dream
while crushing its face against your chest

오래된 일

네가 나를 슬몃 바라보자

나는 떨면서 고개를 수그렸다

어린 연두 물빛이 네 마음의 가녘에서

숨을 가두며 살랑거렸는지도

오래된 일

봄저녁 어두컴컴해서

주소 없는 꽃엽서들은 가버리고

벗 없이 마신 술은

눈썹에 든 애면 꽃술에 어려

네 눈이 바라보던

내 눈의 뿌연 거울은

하냥 먼 너머로 사라졌네

눈동자의 시절

모든 죽음이 살아나는 척하던

지독한 봄날의 일

그리고 오래된 일

It Was a Long Time Ago

While you stealthily gazed at me
I lowered my head and quivered
Perhaps chartreuse water holding its breath
swirled in the corner of your mind
It was a long time ago
The spring evening was pitch-dark
postcards of homeless flowers were censored
and the drink I had by myself
took form as innocent pistils laid on my eyelashes
so as your eyes were gazing into
the cloudy mirrors in my eyes they
evaporated beyond the farthest distance
Days of eyes
All death pretended resurrection
It was an extreme spring thing
and it was a long time ago

포도나무를 태우며

서는 것과 앉는 것 사이에는 아무것도 없습니까
삶과 죽음의 사이는 어떻습니까
어느 해 포도나무는 숨을 멈추었습니다

사이를 알아볼 수 없을 만큼 살았습니다
우리는 건강보험도 없이 늙었습니다
너덜너덜 목 없는 빨래처럼 말라갔습니다

알아볼 수 있어 너무나 사무치던 몇몇 얼굴이 우리의
시간이었습니까
내가 당신을 죽였다면 나는 살아 있습니까
어느 날 창공을 올려다보면서 터뜨릴 울분이 아직도
있습니까

그림자를 뒤에 두고 상처뿐인 발이 혼자 가고 있는 걸
보고 있습니다
그리고 물어봅니다

Burning a Grapevine

Does nothing exist between standing and sitting?
Is there a gap between life and death?
One year a grapevine stopped breathing

We have lived too long to recognize the gap
have become old without health insurance
have become dried like faceless tattered laundry

We recognize some faces that sank deeply into our
hearts
Do they belong to our time?
If I had killed you would I be alive?
Some days do you look into the sky with more an-
ger to vent?

I watch crooked footsteps go on alone leaving the
shadow behind
Then I ask
Did the grapevine's time exist before it was born?
Do we call that the time before the grapevine was
born?

포도나무의 시간은 포도나무가 생기기 전에도 있었습니까

그 시간을 우리는 포도나무가 생기기 전의 시간이라고 부릅니까

지금 타들어가는 포도나무의 시간은 무엇으로 불립니까

정거장에서 이별을 하던 두 별 사이에도 죽음과 삶만이 있습니까

지금 타오르는 저 불길은 무덤입니까 술 없는 음복입니까

그걸 알아볼 수 없어서 우리 삶은 초라합니까

가을달이 지고 있습니다

What do we call this time as the grapevine is burning?

Do only life and death exist between two worlds separating in a train station?

Is this burning flame a grave? Is it *eumbok*[8] with nothing to drink?

Are our lives trivial because we can't recognize them?

The autumn moon is setting

---

8 Korean family members share food and drink at the conclusion of a ritual to commemorate their ancestors.

이 가을의 무늬

아마도 그 병 안에 우는 사람이 들어 있었는지 우는 얼굴을 안아주던 손이 붉은 저녁을 따른다 지난여름을 촘촘히 짜내던 빛은 이제 여름의 무늬를 풀어내기 시작했다

올해 가을의 무늬가 정해질 때까지 빛은 오래 고민스러웠다 그때면,

내가 너를 생각하는 순간 나는 너를 조금씩 잃어버렸다 이해한다고 말하는 순간 너를 절망스런 눈빛의 그림자에 사로잡히게 했다 내 잘못이라고 말하는 순간 세계는 뒤돌아섰다

만지면 만질수록 부풀어 오르는 검푸른 짐승의 울음 같았던 여름의 무늬들이 풀어져서 저 술병 안으로 들어갔다 그리고 새로운 무늬의 시간이 올 때면,

The Pattern of Autumn

Perhaps a crying person was inside the bottle
Hands that embraced the crying face poured out the
red evening   The elaborate light weaving the last of
summer began to unwind the summer patterns

The light had been concerned for a long time until
the patterns of this autumn could be chosen   During
that time

the moment I thought of you I gradually lost you
The moment I said I understood you I captured you in
the shadow of hopeless eyes   The moment I admit-
ted it was my fault the world turned its back to me

The patterns of summer were a dark blue beast
whose cries grew louder the more I touched it   Patterns were unwound inside the bottle of alcohol
When it is time for new patterns

you visit hesitantly behind the crying person's back

너는 아주 돌아올 듯 망설이며 우는 자의 등을 방문한
다 낡은 외투를 그의 등에 슬쩍 올려준다 그는 네가 다
녀간 걸 눈치챘을까? 그랬을 거야, 그랬을 거야 저렇게
툭툭, 털고 다시 가네

오므린 손금처럼 어스름한 가냘픈 길, 그 길이 부셔서
마침내 사월 때까지 보고 있어야겠다 이제 취한 물은
내 손금 안에서 속으로 울음을 오그린 자줏빛으로 흐르
겠다 그것이 이 가을의 무늬겠다

as if not sure you want to come back   You furtively
drape an old coat across his shoulders   Does the
person notice you?   Maybe so   Maybe so   He taps
his fingers to dust off his shoulders and again starts
to go

  The path is dusky and feeble as a line on a cupped
palm   I will observe it until it flares up and finally
burns out   Afterwards drunken waters will stain my
palm lines purple as the tears are held in   That will
be the pattern of autumn

연필 한 자루

그렸다

꿈꾸던 돌의 얼굴을 그렸다

하수구에 머리를 박고 거꾸로 서 있던 백양목

부서진 벽 앞에 서서 누군가를 기다리던 어깨

붉게 울면서 태양과 결별하던 자두를 그렸다

칼에 목을 내밀며 검은 중심을 숲에서 나오게 하고 싶
었다

짧아진다는 거, 목숨의 한 순간을 내미는 거

정치도 박애도 아니고 깨달음도 아니고

다만 당신을 향해 나를 건다는 거

멸종해가던 거대 짐승의 목

먹다 남은 생선 머리 뼈 꼬리 마침내 차가운 눈

열대림이 눈을 감으며 아무도 모르는 부족의 노래를
듣는 거

태양이 들판에 정주하던 안개를 밀어내던 거

천천히 몸을 낮추며 쓰러지는 너를 바라보던 오래된
노래

Pencil

drew

drew the face of a dreaming stone

drew an aspen tree standing upside down with its
head in a ditch

shoulders waiting for someone in front of a collapsed wall

a plum shedding red tears as it broke up with the
sun

With a knife against the neck

wanted to take the black core from out of the woods

Growing shorter but protruding a moment of life

not for politics nor philanthropy nor enlightenment

I staked myself only for you

drew

the neck of the huge disappearing beast

leftover fish head bones tails and finally dead eyes

a tropical forest hearing an unknown tribe's songs
as it closed its eyes

sun shoving the settling fog away from the field

the old song gazing at you as you slowly collapsed

눈물 머금은 비닐봉지도 그 봉지의 아들들이

화염병의 신음으로 만든 반지를 끼는 거

어둠에 매장당하는 나무를 보는 거

사랑을 배반하던 순간, 섬뜩섬뜩 위장으로 들어가던
찬물

늦여름의 만남, 그 상처의 얼굴을 닮아가면서 익는 오
렌지를

그렸다

마침내 필통도 그를 매장할 때쯤

이 세계 전체가 관이 되는 연필이었다, 우리는

점점 짧아지면서 떠나온 어머니를 생각했으나

영영 생각나지 않았다

우리는 단독자, 연필 한 자루였다

헤어질 사람들이 히말라야에서 발원한 물에서

영원한 목욕을 하는 것을 지켜보며

그것이 음악이라고 생각하는 한 자루였다

당신이여, 그것뿐이었다

and lay down your body

   sons wearing tear-filled plastic bags over their faces

   wearing jewelry made from the groans of the Molo-
tov cocktails

   watching a tree being buried in darkness

   the moment love was betrayed   the cold water fill-
ing the stomach in chills   meeting a late summer
an orange ripening to resemble the wounded face

   When it was finally time the pencil case would bury
him

   the whole world felt like a coffin to the pencil   We

   tried to think of mothers left behind as we grew
shorter

   but we could never remember

   We were a single person   a pencil

   We were a pencil who believed it was music

   as we watched people eternally bathing

   in the waters from the Himalayas although they
must be separated

   Dear you   that was all

돌이킬 수 없었다

언젠가
돌이킬 수 없는 일이 있었다
치욕스럽다, 할 것까지는 아니었으나
쉽게 잊힐 일도 아니었다

흐느끼면서
혼자 떠나버린 나의 가방은
돌아오지 않았다

비가 오는 것도 아니었는데
머리칼은 젖어서
감기가 든 영혼은 자주 콜록거렸다

누런 아기를 손마디에 달고 흔들거리던 은행나무가
물었다, 나, 때문인가요?
쳄로의 아픈 손가락을 쓸어주던 바람이 물었다, 나,
때문인가요?

Irreversible

Once
an irreversible thing occurred
It wasn't humiliating but
it also wasn't something so easily forgotten

Weeping
my bag left on its on
and never returned

It wasn't raining
yet my hair got drenched
so my soul caught a cold with a chronic cough

A gingko tree swaying with yellow babies hanging
from its knuckles asked
Me, am I to blame?
The wind rubbing the aching fingers on a cello asked
Me, am I to blame?
A middle-aged singer silently changing out of stage
clothes backstage asked

무대 뒤편에서 조용히 의상을 갈아입던 중년 가수가
물었다, 나 때문인가요?

누구 때문도 아니었다
말 못 할 일이었으므로
고개를 흔들며 그들을 보냈다

시간이 날 때마다 터미널로 나가
돌아오지 않는 가방을 기다렸다

술냄새가 나는 오래된 날씨를 누군가
매일매일 택배로 보내왔다

마침내 터미널에서
불가능과 비슷한 온도를 가진
우동 국물을 넘겼다

가방은 영원히 돌아오지 않을 거라는
예감 때문이었다
그 예감은 참, 무참히 돌이킬 수 없었다

Am I to blame?

It was nobody's fault
It wasn't possible to explain why
so shaking my head I released them

Whenever I found the time I went to the bus terminal
and waited for my bag that never returned

Everyday someone sent me
a parcel of old weather that reeked of alcohol

Finally in the terminal
I swallowed *udon*[9] soup
which had a temperature similar to impossibility

Because I had a hunch
my bag would never return
That hunch was really, tragically irreversible

---

9 A thick wheat noodle common in Japanese cuisine.

우산을 만지작거리며

우산을 만지작거리며 아무 데도 가지 않았다 삶과 연애 중이라고 생각하라고 심리상담사는 말했다 우산을 만지작거리며 나가볼까 생각한다 생계를 위해서라면 나가야 한다고 생각한다

먹는 것보다 자는 것이 중요하다고 심리상담사는 말했다 사는 것보다 죽는 것이 더 중요하다고 말했더라면 이해할 수 있었을 것이다 나는 가끔 심리상담사를 죽이는 꿈을 꾸다가 그가 내 얼굴을 달고 있는 장면에서 꼭 잠을 깬다 내 얼굴을 향하여 내가 칼을 들이밀고 있었으므로

그때 그 어느 날 심리상담사에게 죽은 허 씨에게, 라고 시작되는 편지를 보여주지 말아야 했다 얼어 죽은 국회에게, 라는 편지도 맞아 죽은 은행에게, 우주로 납치된 악몽에게, 달에 있는 나의 거대한 저택에게, 라고 시작되는 편지도 어떤 편지도, 아니 내가 끊임없이 편지를 쓰는 식물이라고 고백하지 않는 편이 나았다

Fiddling with an Umbrella

Fiddling with an umbrella I didn't go anywhere
The shrink said I should believe I'm in love with my
life   Fiddling with an umbrella I think about getting
out   I think I should get out to make a living

The shrink says sleep's more important than food
I could get it if he says dying's more important than
living   Sometimes I dream about killing the shrink
but just at that moment he's wearing my face   You
bet I wake up   And I'm pointing a knife at my own
face

At that day at that time I shouldn't have shown the
shrink the letter with the greeting *Dear dead Ms. Huh*
Or the one starting *Dear fucked-up Senators* or the
other letters going *Dear gingko tree beaten to death,
Dear nightmare kidnapped by the cosmos, Dear huge
mansion in the moon* or any letter at all, no, it would
have been best if I hadn't confessed that I'm only a
plant that can't stop writing letters

나는 동물의 말을 하는 식물입니다
나는 희망의 말을 하는 신입니다
나는 유곽의 말을 하는 관공서입니다
나는 시계의 말을 하는 시간입니다
나는 개가 꾸는 꿈입니다
등등의 고백도 하지 않는 편이 나았다

하지만 고백하고 말았다(물론 나는 그걸 강제된 고백이라
고 부르고 싶기는 하다) 나라는 나쁜 인간을 방어할 무기가
나에게는 필요하다 나를 공허하게 버려줄 무기가 너에
게는 필요하다

우산을 만지작거리며 오늘 오후에 있는 그와의 약속
을 생각한다 불투명한 유리가 끼워진 대기실도 대기실
에 붙여둔 자살 위험이 있는 사람들의 일곱 가지 특징
에 대해서도 내가 읽어보면 그들은 다 살지 못해서 안
달한 사람인데 심리상담사의 꼬임 혹은 그의 인턴이 건
네주던 하얀 줄이 박힌 푸른 사탕 때문에 나처럼 고백
을 한 사람들일 뿐인데

우산을 만지작거리며
나는 웃는다 울 일이 없어서 심란한 아이 같다

I'm a plant speaking animal languages

I'm a god speaking the language of hope

I'm a government office speaking the red light dis-
trict's language

I'm time speaking the language of a clock

I'm the dream a dog dreams

Etc.   It would have been best if I hadn't confessed

But I confessed (Of course I believe it was coerced)

I'm so bad I need a weapon to defend myself   You
better get a weapon if you're going to leave me hollow

Fiddling with an umbrella I think of the afternoon
appointment with my shrink and the waiting room
decor of frosted glass and the seven types of suicidal
people on that poster in the waiting room   It all
seems to me like dying to live and they're just people
like me who confessed because the shrink got them
to or they were tempted by the blue candy with
white stripes that his intern offered

Fiddling with an umbrella

I laugh   I look like a child who's upset because
there's no reason to cry

출처

「혼자 가는 먼 집」: 『혼자 가는 먼 집』, 문학과지성사, 1992

「불취불귀」: 『혼자 가는 먼 집』, 문학과지성사, 1992

「공터의 사랑」: 『혼자 가는 먼 집』, 문학과지성사, 1992

「흰 꿈 한 꿈」: 『혼자 가는 먼 집』, 문학과지성사, 1992

「너의 눈 속에 나는 있다」: 『빌어먹을, 차가운 심장』, 문학동네, 2011

「글로벌 블루스 2009」: 『빌어먹을, 차가운 심장』, 문학동네, 2011

「비행장을 떠나면서」: 『빌어먹을, 차가운 심장』, 문학동네, 2011

「차가운 해가 뜨거운 발을 굴릴 때」: 『빌어먹을, 차가운 심장』, 문학동네, 2011

「아름다운 나날」: 『빌어먹을, 차가운 심장』, 문학동네, 2011

「그때 낙타가 들어왔다」: 『빌어먹을, 차가운 심장』, 문학동네, 2011

「빌어먹을, 차가운 심장」: 『빌어먹을, 차가운 심장』, 문학동네, 2011

「레몬」: 『누구도 기억하지 않는 역에서』, 문학과지성사, 2016

「수박」: 『누구도 기억하지 않는 역에서』, 문학과지성사, 2016

「딸기」: 『누구도 기억하지 않는 역에서』, 문학과지성사, 2016

「오래된 일」: 『누구도 기억하지 않는 역에서』, 문학과지성사, 2016

「포도나무를 태우며」: 『누구도 기억하지 않는 역에서』, 문학과지성사, 2016

「이 가을의 무늬」: 『누구도 기억하지 않는 역에서』, 문학과지성사, 2016

「연필 한 자루」: 『누구도 기억하지 않는 역에서』, 문학과지성사, 2016

「돌이킬 수 없었다」: 『누구도 기억하지 않는 역에서』, 문학과지성사, 2016

「우산을 만지작거리며」: 『누구도 기억하지 않는 역에서』, 문학과지성사, 2016

시인노트
Poet's Note

POET

오래 전 지금 사는 집으로 이사를 했을 때 부엌 한 귀퉁이에 뒹굴고 있던 십자가를 발견한 적이 있다. 황동으로 만들어진 오 센티미터쯤 되는 작은 십자가였는데 아마도 전 주인이 잊어버리고 챙기지 못한 모양이었다. 나는 기독교인이 아니다. 하지만 십자가를 내 것이 아니라고 해서 쓰레기통에 버릴 수는 없었다. 누군가, 이 작은 십자가에 의지해서 어두운 시간을 밝혀내려고 했을 것이기 때문이다. 십자가를 나는 내 책상서랍 안에 넣어두었고 잊어버렸다. 그러던 어느 날, 무언가에 의지하지 않으면 살아내기 힘든 지경까지 삶에 불행이 찾아왔을 때 우연히 십자가를 책상서랍 안에서 발견했다. 나는 그십자가를 손에 들고 아주 오랫동안 들여다보았다. 간절한 마음으로 고난과 불행을 견뎌내던 한 사람, 어떤 연

When I moved into this house a long time ago, I found a cross that had been dropped carelessly in the corner of the kitchen. It was about five centimeters and was made of brass. Perhaps the former owner forgot it. I'm not a Christian, but I couldn't dump it in the trash because it wasn't mine. I realized someone had tried to light up dark hours by relying on this tiny cross. I put the cross in my desk drawer and forgot about it. Then one day, I suffered a huge misfortune and desperately needed something to rely on, and I happened to find the cross in the drawer. For a long time, I held it in my hand and gazed at it, thinking about the person who had endured sorrows with an

유인지는 모르겠지만 그 사람이 잊어버리고 가버린 십자가. 하지만 그 사람이 잊어버린 십자가를 발견한 다른 사람은 그 십자가를 붙들고 있다. 위로를 받으려고 했는지 희망을 발견하려 했는지 나는 알지 못한다. 다만 십자가를 들고 물끄러미 바라보며 전 주인이 십자가와 함께 보냈던 시간을 상상해보는 것이 위로가 되었다.

시를 쓰던 순간은 어쩌면 그렇게 다른 이가 잊어버리고 간 십자가를 바라보는 일인지도 모른다. 십자가라는 것이 한 종교에 속한 상징이라면 다른 종교에 속한 어떤 상징도 마찬가지이다. 간절한 한 사람의 시간을 붙들고 있는 것, 그 시간을 공감하는 것, 그것은 시를 쓰는 마음이라는 생각을 나는 하곤 한다. 사람의 시간뿐 아닐 것이다. 어린 수국 한 그루를 마당에 심어놓고 아침저녁으로 바라보는 일도 그와 다르지 않을 것이다. 아기 새들이 종일 지저귀던 늙은 전나무에 있는 새집을 바라보던 시간도 마찬가지일 것이다. 간절한 어느 순간이 가지는 강렬한 사랑을 향한 힘. 그것이 시를 쓰는 시간일 것이다. 시를 쓰는 순간 그것 자체가 가진 힘이 시인을 시인으로 살아가게 할 것이다.

earnest prayer but for some reason had gone away and left the cross behind. Now another person had found and was holding it. I don't know if I expected to find some comfort, or if I was trying to find hope, but simply gazing at the cross in my hand and thinking about its former owner gave me some consolation.

The act of writing a poem may be the same as looking upon a cross someone has left behind. Symbols unrelated to religion are similar. I sometimes think considering a person's earnest experiences, and empathizing with those times are the heart of writing poetry. It works with non-human experiences as well; watching a little hydrangea tree in the yard during mornings and evenings is the same. Observing a nest in an old fir tree, with little birds twittering all day long is the same. An earnest moment holds the power of intense love. That may be the time of writing poetry. At that moment, the power of the act lets a poet live as a poet.

해설
Commentary

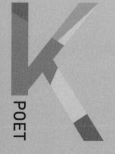

상처는 어떻게 사랑이 되는가

허수경의 시는 상처와 울음으로 빚은 사랑의 세레나데다. 하지만 사랑의 고백을 들어줄 애인은 떠나고 없고, 그녀는 가난하여 연주할 악기조차 하나 없다. 그녀가 가진 것은 울음 속에 "킥킥거리며" 겨우 발성하는 자신의 갈라지고 쉰 목소리뿐이다. 허수경은 아무도 없는 텅 빈 '공터'나, 언제 도착할지 모를 '먼 집'으로 가는 쓸쓸한 길에서 사랑을 노래한다. 혼자, "환하고 아픈 자리로 가"(「공터의 사랑」)서 부르는 사랑 노래는 '당신'의 부재와 '나'의 상실감을 더 깊게 만든다. '내'가 연주하는 것이 노래인지 신음인지, '내'가 내는 소리가 울음인지 웃음인지 구별하기 힘들다.

How Can Wounds Become Love?

Kim Suyee(literary Critic)

Huh Soo-kyung's poetry is a serenade composed of wounds and tears. However, the lover who was supposed to hear her declaration of love has left her, and she is too poor to own any musical instrument to play. The only thing she owns is her cracked and hoarse voice that she barely uses, "giggling" through her tears. Huh sings about "love in an empty lot," or on the street while she walks alone to "a distant home" where she doesn't know when she will get to. When the speaker goes "to that bright hurting spot" (from "Love in an Empty Lot") and sings a love song alone, *your* absence becomes deeper and *my* feeling of loss gets worse. It is hard to tell whether *I* play a song or groan;

허수경은 노래와 신음, 울음과 웃음이 뒤섞인 독특한 발성법으로 한국의 독자들을 강렬하게 사로잡았다. 그녀의 시가 뿜어내는 환하고도 아픈 빛은, 흐르는 눈물 속에 반짝이는 엷은 미소처럼 하나의 단어로 표현할 수 없는 복합적인 감정을 불러일으킨다. 초기시에서 허수경은 이 감정을 주로 '봄'의 계열 이미지들로 표현했다. 공터에 비치는 환하고도 시린 봄 햇살, '당신'과 예전에 만난 곳에 드리워 있던 봄 그늘 등은, 한국시에서 '낡은 것'으로 여겨지던 전통적인 '정한(情恨)'의 정서를 현재형으로 생생히 일깨웠다. 20세기가 끝나기 십 년 전쯤의 일이었다. 나중에 허수경은 그 시절을 이렇게 회상한다. "네가 나를 슬몃 바라보자/나는 떨면서 고개를 수그렸다/ (…) / 모든 죽음이 살아나는 척하던/지독한 봄날의 일/그리고 오래된 일"(「오래된 일」).

'정한'은 따뜻한 정과 슬픔, 사랑과 원망 등의 양가적이며 동시적인 감정을 아우르는 말이다. 외국어로 번역하기 힘든 한국의 독특한 정서를 가리킨다. 허수경은 한국인의 가슴에 전해 내려오는 오래된 정서와 가락을 현대의 일상 속에 되살렸다. 허수경의 시를 통해 독자들은 자신의 마음속 '상처와 울음'이 먼 옛날로부터 이

whether the speaker is crying or laughing.

Huh's unique vocalized mixture of singing and groaning, crying and laughing has intensely attracted Korean readers. The bright and hurting light that her poetry radiates evokes a complex feeling that cannot be expressed with one word, like a little smile glittering in tears. In her earlier poems of the 1990s she expressed this feeling mostly with images of spring, such as dazzling spring sunlight shining in an empty lot and spring shadows in the place where *I* used to meet *you*. This revives the traditional Korean sentiment of *jeonghan*, which had been considered old-fashioned in modern Korean poetry, vividly into the present. Later, she recalled those days: "While you stealthily gazed at me/I lowered my head and quivered ⋯ All death pretended resurrection/It was an extreme spring thing/and it was a long time ago" (from "It Was a Long Time Ago").

Jeonghan is almost untranslatable to non-Koreans; the portmanteau expression contains the ambivalent feelings of *jeong* (a love relationship but also responsibility) and *han* (sorrow, but also blame). Huh presents these old familiar sentiments and melodies, which are inherited in Koreans' hearts, in modern routines.

어져 온 정서와 가락으로 편곡 되는 경험을 했다. 그 선율은 깊은 내면의 상처와 울음에 어떤 음악보다도 어울리는 것이었다. 두 번째 시집 『혼자 가는 먼 집』을 출간한 1992년에 한국을 떠난 허수경은, 현재까지 독일에서 살면서 이 작업을 계속해 오고 있다.

허수경의 시는 '상처와 울음의 한국적인 고고학이자 음악이며 미학'이다. 그러나 허수경은 '과거'에 매료된 시인이 아니라, '현재'가 지닌 오래된 것의 깊이를 살아내는 시인이다. 허수경에게 중요한 것은 단지 현재 자체가 아니라, 현재의 깊이이며 역사이다. 같은 맥락에서 '현재의 나' 자체가 아니라, '현재의 나'가 지닌 깊이이며 세월이다. 허수경은 '나'라는 인간 존재의 고고학과, 이를 현재 속에서 미학적으로 처리하는 방식을 개발하는 데 몰두한다. 그녀가 독일로 떠난 이유가 선사고고학을 공부하기 위해서였던 것은 우연이 아니었다.

허수경과 허수경 시의 '나'는 현대 도시에서 살아가는 생활인이다. '나'는 도시의 삭막한 거리를 걷고, 허름한 식당에서 서러운 밥 한 끼를 먹으며, 떠난 사랑과 고달픈 생계에 눈앞이 캄캄해지곤 한다. '당신'이 '나'를 떠났는데도 — 어쩌면 '당신'이 '나'를 떠난 까닭에

Through her poems, Korean readers experience the wounds and tears in their mind arranged as the emotions and lyrics from the country's long history. The lyrics do more to heal the inner wounds and tears than any other music. She continues to express Korean values even after moving to Germany to study prehistoric archeology in 1992 when she published her second poetry book, *I Go Alone to A Distant Home*.

Huh Soo-kyung's poetry is a Korean style of archeology, music and aesthetics of wounds and tears. She, however, is not fascinated by the past; instead, she lives the depth of old things that the present contains. The important thing to her is not the present itself but the depth and the history of the present. In the same sense, it is not *present me* itself but the depth and the time that *present me* retains. She is absorbed in the archeology of the existence of self and is also immersed in developing the way to treat it aesthetically inside the present.

The speakers in Huh's poems are people living in modern cities. They walk on the dreary street of a city, have a meal in a cheap restaurant, feel sorrow, and fully feel despair from lost loves and the hardships of poverty. Even though *you* left *me*

─, '나'는 '당신'과 평생을 동행한다. 나는 떠난 당신을 내 "마음의 무덤"에 묻었다. 나는 당신을 잃고 마음이 죽은 자이며, 마음의 무덤에 제사를 지내며 죽은 내 마음을 애도하는 자이다. "금방 울 것 같은 사내의 아름다움 그 아름다움에 기대 마음의 무덤에 나 벌초하러 진설 음식도 없이 맨 술 한 병 차고 병자처럼". "당신이라는 말 참 좋지요, 내가 아니라서 끝내 버릴 수 없는, 무를 수도 없는 참혹……"(「혼자 가는 먼 집」). 당신을 버릴 수도 무를 수도 없기에, 애도는 완성될 수 없다. 나는 마음이 죽은 자이며, 죽은 나의 마음을 애도하는 자이다. 죽음과 애도를 동시에 행해야 하는 나는 온전히 살아 있지도 죽어 있지도 않다. 나는 병자, 술에 취한 자, 잠들어 꿈꾸는 자, 늙은이다. 인생은 한낱 꿈과 같고, 나는 그 헛된 꿈속에서 술에 취해 죽어간다. "몽생취사"(「不醉不歸」)다. 허수경은 '취생몽사'(醉生夢死, 술에 취해 잠들어 꾸는 꿈속에서 살고 죽는다는 뜻으로, 아무 하는 일 없이 한평생을 흐리멍덩하게 살아감을 비유한 말.)를 패러디해 이 말을 만들었다.

내가 살아내지 않아도 세월은 흐른다. 상실과 고통은 인간의 몫일 뿐, 세월의 몫이 아니다. 흐르는 세월 속에

or perhaps because *you* left *me*—*I* live together with *you* forever. *I* buried *you* who left in "the grave of my mind" (from "I Go Alone to a Distant Home"). *I* lost *you* and *my* mind died, and *I* grieve its death, having a ritual at its grave:

The beauty of a guy near tears, leaning on that beauty I head to the grave of my mind to cut the weeds with only a bottle of alcohol hanging from my hip and no food to arrange at the grave   Like a sick person⋯ the word 'you' sounds so good because it isn't me   I can never abandon the misery or ask for a refund⋯ (from "I Go Alone to a Distant Home")

I can't abandon *you* and ask for a refund, so the mourning can't be completed. *I* am both the person whose mind died and the person who mourns for it. As the person who should grieve the death of the mind, I am neither completely alive nor dead. *I* am a sick person, a drunken person, a sleeper having a dream, or an old person. Life is just like a dream, and *I* "die drunkenly, living in a dream" (from "Bul-Chwi-Bulg-Wi").

Even though *I* don't try to live, time still flows. Loss

서 내 마음의 "검은 무덤"에 묻힌 사랑의 시체는 부패한다. "한참 동안 그대로 있었다/썩었는가 사랑아"(「공터의 사랑」). 잃어버린 것에 대한 애도는 시의 보편적인 주제이지만, 허수경의 시는 독특한 애도의 언어와 미학으로 한국시에 잊을 수 없는 목소리를 남긴다. 애초에 허수경의 시적 목표는 애도를 끝내는 것이 아니라, 세상의 모든 "환하고 아픈 자리로 가"서 애도를 계속하는 것이었다. "잊혀진 상처의 늙은 자리는 환하다/환하고 아프다//환하고 아픈 자리로 가리라/앓는 꿈이 다시 세월을 얻을 때"(「공터의 사랑」). 어느덧 허수경에게 애도는 그 자체로 사랑의 행위가 된다. 애도와 사랑은 이제 같은 서술어를 공유한다. 상처도, 애도도, 사랑도, 그리고 당신과 나도 모두 "환하고 아프다".

허수경은 애도의 대상을 그녀가 혼자 잃은 것에 한정하지 않는다. 허수경은 현대의 자연과 문명이 각기 잃어버렸으되 공동체 전체의 손실이 된 것들로 시야를 넓힌다. "우리는 단독자"(「연필 한 자루」)이지만, '상실한 존재'이며 '상처받은 존재'라는 동일한 정체성을 지닌 단독자다. 시 「너의 눈 속에 나는 있다」, 「차가운 해가 뜨거운 발을 굴릴 때」 등에서 허수경은 그 목록을 예시한

and pain are humans' fate, not time's. In flowing time, the corpse of love buried in the "black graves" of the mind rots. "After being still for so long/has love rotted?"(from "Love in an Empty Lot"). Grieving over loss is a universal theme of poetry, but Huh's poems present an indelible voice with the unique language of grieving and aesthetics in Korean poetry. From the very beginning, the purpose of her poetry was not to finish grieving, but to continue it. "An old scar from a forgotten wound is bright/Bright and hurting//I will go to that bright hurting spot/at the instant the ill dream is revived" (from "Love in an Empty Lot"). Before realization, for Huh, grief itself becomes the action of love. Now grief and love share the same predicate. Wound, grief, love, and *you* and *me*, all are "Bright and hurting."

Huh doesn't restrict the objects for grieving to her own losses. She broadens her horizons to what modern nature and civilization respectively have lost, which became the losses of the whole community. "We were a single person" (from "Pencil") but we all are single people with the same identity that is the *person who lost things* and the *person who got hurt*. She lists the objects in her poems like "I Exist

다. 도심에서 차에 치이는 다람쥐, 내일이면 도살될 돼지들, 저녁 퇴근길 답답한 차 안에서 고함을 치는 너, 먼 열대에서 오래된 노래를 흥얼거리며 뻘게를 찾는 작은 남자와 그의 아이들, 공원에서 술병을 들고 앉아 있는 늙은 남자 등. '당신'을 잃어버린 '나'는 이제 세상의 수많은 타자들, 특히 약자들 속에서 자신을 재발견한다. "컴컴한 곳에서 아주 작은 빛이 나올 때/너의 눈빛 그 속에 나는 있다/미약한 약속의 생이었다". 이 미약한 약속의 이름은 '사랑'이다.

상처와 상실로 빚은 허수경의 '사랑'은 개인과 공동체의 현실을 넘어, 근대의 역사 전체를 관통하는 열쇠가 된다. 허수경은 근대의 역사를 "이름 없는 섬들에 살던 많은 짐승들이 죽어가는 세월"(「빌어먹을, 차가운 심장」)이라고 규정한다. "이름 없는 것들"이 "이름 없는 세월" 속에 죽어가는 근대는 비인간적인 시스템과 비극적인 사건들을 끝없이 쏟아낸다. 이것은 "긴 세기의 이야기"이며, "빌어먹을, 차가운 심장의 이야기"이다. 허수경은 근대의 역사가 '이름'을 빼앗기고 '목소리(권리)'를 빼앗겨 상실을 말하지 못하는 자들의 이야기임을 간파한다. 상실보다는, 상실을 말하지 못하는 것이 더 혹독

Inside Your Eyes" and "When the Cold Sun Shifts His Hot Feet." A squirrel run over by a car while rushing across the downtown street, a pig to be slaughtered tomorrow, you who yell at the top of your lungs in your car on the way home in the evening rush hour, a short guy and his kids who hum an old song as they search for three-spined crabs on the shore, and the old guy sitting with a bottle in a park, and so on. *I* who lost *you* rediscover self from many others in the world, especially from the weak. "When the slightest light gleams from a pitch-dark place/I exist inside the expression of your eyes/It is the life of a faint promise" (from "I Exist Inside Your Eyes"). The name of this faint promise is love.

Huh shapes love with wounds and loss that rises above the reality of individuals and the community to become the key piercing all modern history. She defines modern history as "days when many animals on nameless islands are dying" (from "Damn My Cold Heart"). The modern times when nameless things are dying on nameless islands generate inhumane systems and tragedies without stopping. This is "a story of a long century" and "a story of damn my cold heart" (from "Damn My Cold Heart"). She detects mod-

한 상처다. 상실을 말하지 못하는 곳에서는 사랑도 추방된다. 허수경이 일찍이 통찰한 바와 같이, 상실의 언어는 사랑의 언어와 서술어가 같다. 상실도 사랑도 "환하고 아프다". 당신을 잃고 울어 온 '나'는, 이제 '당신'이 도처에서 울고 있음을 본다.

> 아님, 말 못하는 것들이라 영혼이 없다고 말하던
> 근대 입구의 세월 속에
> 당신, 아직도 울고 있나요?
> ─「빌어먹을, 차가운 심장」 중에서

상실을 말할 수 없는 '당신'들로 가득한 근대의 이야기에는 결정적으로 부족한 것은 '사랑'이다. 근대사회가 양산하는 폭력적인 상실들을 '사랑'으로 바꾸기 위해서는 얼마나 많은 '환한 빛'이 필요한 것일까. 허수경은 그 일을 감당하는 것이 근대시의 운명이며, 근대적 시인의 소명이라고 생각하는 듯하다. 그녀의 시가 "기적처럼" 발견해 우리에게 전해주는 아프고 환한 빛이 그 증거로 우리 앞에 있다.

> 이제는 당신의 저만치 가 있는 마음도 좋아요

ern history as the story of those who have lost their names and voices (rights), so they can't vocalize their loss. Being unable to vocalizing loss is a more horrible pain than loss itself. In the place where loss can't be expressed, love is exiled. Like the insight Huh obtained early, the language of loss has the same predicate as the predicate of the language of love. Both loss and love are "bright and hurting." The *I* who has been crying after losing *you* now witnesses *you* crying everywhere.

> Or, on days at the threshold of modern times
> that said mutes don't have souls
> Hey you, still crying?
>
> from "Damn My Cold Heart"

Love is the crucially insufficient thing in the story of modern times full of those who can't verbalize loss. How much bright light is needed to change violent loss, which modern society massively produces, into love? Huh seems to think that being equal to this task is the fate and calling of modern poetry. The bright hurting light that her poems discover is unmistakable evidence.

내가 어떻게 보았을까요, 기적처럼 이제 곧

　　푸르게 차오르는 냇물의 시간이 온다는 걸
　　가재와 붕장어의 시간이 온다는 걸
　　선잠과 어린 새벽의 손이 포플러처럼 흔들리는 시간
이 온다는 걸
　　날아가는 어린 새가 수박빛 향기를 물고 가는 시간이
온다는 걸

- 「수박」 중에서

now I like your detached mind too

How could I see it? As quickly as a miracle

the time of a stream swelling in blue will come
the time of crayfish and congers will come
the time of shallow sleep and tiny hands of dawn swaying like poplar leaves will come
the time of a little bird flying with a watermelon-tinted
fragrance in its beak will come

From "Watermelon"

허수경에
대해

What They Say
About Huh Sukyung

POET

자신만의 고유한 울림을 우리에게 인상 깊게 각인 시켜온 허수경의 시는 자기 자신을 답습하지 않고 끊임없이 자기 자신 너머에 대해 질문하기를 멈추지 않는다는 점에서도 큰 신뢰와 무한한 애정을 갖게 한다. 와르르 무너지게 한다. 환하고 아프게 한다. 통과하게 한다. 마음을 상처를 사랑을 자신을 ……모국어 바깥에서 살아가야 하는 숙명 속에서 모국어를 지문처럼 새긴 그의 시는 차라리 시가 된 '심장'이다.

안현미

허수경의 시는 일상의 비애 가운데서도 자기 연민에

Huh Sukyung's poems have made a good impression on us with her own echoes. They also give us much trust and endless affection because she doesn't easily accept or follow herself, instead, ceaselessly asks questions about going beyond herself, making us crash and feel bright and hurting. They let us pass through our minds, wounds, loves, ourselves... Her poetry, written in her mother tongue that is engraved like finger prints in the fate that she should live outside her mother land, is "the heart" that became poetry.

An Heon-Mi

빠지지 않고, 인류 자체의 감각과 정면으로 마주한 채 세계의 운명과 대결하려는 순간들로 가득하다. 그것은 고고학이나 디아스포라처럼 단순화된 기표로 유추되는 게 아니라, 시간의 절대성과 공간의 상대성 속에 놓인 인간의 고통과 결핍을 존재론적 증상으로 다룬다는 점에서 특별하다. 그래서 타자의 서사로 맞닥뜨린 전쟁과 궁핍의 역사에 지극히 동참하는 방법으로써 그는 그리움을 노래하고 있다. 이때, 그의 시는 어떤 정치적 타산이 개입할 여지를 남기지 않음으로써 역설적으로 가장 정치적인 한순간을 선보이는데, 이는 일부에서 난해한 문법 속에서만 호명되어왔던 한국시의 다른 가능성을, 인간 자체에 대한 탐구를 통해 제시하는 귀한 사례일 수 있을 것이다.

신용목

그녀가 처음 문단에 나왔을 때, 그 충격은 지금의 여느 스타 못지않았다. 시인은 우리말의 가락을 살린 독특한 어법으로 새로운 관능의 세계를 선보였다. 허수경의 시는 역사의 폐허와 인간의 외로움을 여성의 구슬픈 곡조와 결합시킨다. 취기 가득한 유랑가수의 목소리로

Huh Sukyung's poems don't fall into self-pity even amid the sorrows of daily life, and are full of moments that confront the destiny of the world, facing all mankind's senses. Her poems aren't analogized out of simplified signifiers like archeology or diaspora. They are special because they deal with people's pains and wants that lie in the absoluteness of time and the relativity of space in an ontological perspective. So, she sings our yearnings by extreme participation in the history of wars and poverty she never experienced. Her poetry doesn't leave room for any political calculations. Paradoxically, this creates the most political moment, a very rare case that suggests another possibility to Korean poems that have been written in unnecessarily abstruse grammar, through her quest for humans themselves.

Shin Yong-Mok

Her first appearance in the Korean literary world was shocking. She introduced a new sensual world with her unique mode of expression by enlivening Korean melo-

읊조리는 시. 이것이 허수경의 시였다.

이윤주

허수경의 시 세계를 지탱하는 진정한 힘과 매력은 이 전경의 배후에 깔려 있는 심층의 음화 속에 들어 있는 것으로 보인다. 허수경의 시는 떠도는 영혼의 슬픈 고향상실의 노래인 동시에 또한 삶의 정처 없음을 자신의 정처로 삼은 한 불우한 영혼의 전망 없는 세계에 대한 위대한 연민의 노래인 셈이다.

김진수

dies. Her poems combine ruins of history and human loneliness with female sorrowful tunes. Hers are the poems recited by a fully drunken, wandering singer's voice.

Yi Yoon-Joo

True strength and attraction maintained in Huh Sukyung's poetic world seem to be contained in the film negative of depths which spread behind the foreground. Her poems are sad songs about wandering souls that lost their hometowns, and also about great compassion for the hopeless world of less fortunate people who settled inside their wandering life.

Kim Jin-Soo

K-포엣
허수경 시선

2017년 12월 29일 초판 1쇄 발행
2018년 11월 19일 초판 2쇄 발행

지은이 허수경 | 옮긴이 지영실, 다니엘 토드 파커 | 펴낸이 김재범
기획위원 이영광, 안현미, 김근
편집장 김형욱 | 편집 강민영 | 관리 강초민, 홍희표 | 디자인 나루기획
인쇄·제책 굿에그커뮤니케이션 | 종이 한솔PNS
펴낸곳 (주)아시아 | 출판등록 2006년 1월 27일 제406-2006-000004호
주소 경기도 파주시 회동길 445(서울 사무소: 서울특별시 동작구 서달로 161-1 3층)
전화 02.821.5055 | 팩스 02.821.5057 | 홈페이지 www.bookasia.org
ISBN 979-11-5662-317-5 (set) | 979-11-5662-336-6 (04810)
값은 뒤표지에 있습니다.

K-Poet
Poems by Huh Sukyung

Written by Huh Sukyung | **Translated by** YoungShil Ji, Daniel T. Parker
Published by ASIA Publishers | 445, Hoedong-gil, Paju-si, Gyeonggi-do, Korea
(Seoul Office: 161-1, Seodal-ro, Dongjak-gu, Seoul, Korea)
Homepage Address www.bookasia.org | **Tel** (822).821.5055 | **Fax** (822).821.5057
ISBN 979-11-5662-317-5 (set) | 979-11-5662-336-6 (04810)
First published in Korea by ASIA Publishers 2017

This book is published with the support of the Literature Translation Institute of Korea
(LTI Korea).

K-픽션 한국 젊은 소설

최근에 발표된 단편소설 중 가장 우수하고 흥미로운 작품을 엄선하여 출간하는 〈K-픽션〉은 한국문학의 생생한 현장을 국내외 독자들과 실시간으로 공유하고자 기획되었습니다. 원작의 재미와 품격을 최대한 살린 〈K-픽션〉 시리즈는 매 계절마다 새로운 작품을 선보입니다.